The Life and Times of
Lilly the Lash®

The Kacklin' Kitchen
Written By Julie Woik

Wow!!! Ya Two Are Fantastic!

To Caden & Brynn-
Respect Yourself... Respect Your Neighbor...
Respect Your World!!!
Let's Do Something Really Cool...
Let's Work Together
To Make A Difference!!!!
March 2019
Yahooooo

Snow in Sarasota Publishing, Inc.
Osprey, FL 34229
Library of Congress Cataloging in Publication Data
Woik Julie
The Kacklin' Kitchen
(Book #4 in The Life and Times of Lilly the Lash® series)

p. cm.
ISBN – 978-0-9893840-0-1
1. Fiction, Juvenile 2. Psychology, self-esteem 3. Multi-cultural

First Edition
10 9 8 7 6 5 4 3 2 1

Design: Elsa Kauffman
Illustration: Marc Tobin

Printed by Manatee Printers, Inc., Bradenton, Florida
in the United States of America

ABOUT THIS BOOK

The Life and Times of Lilly the Lash® is a series of fascinating children's books, in which an **EYELASH** teaches life lessons and the importance of strong self-esteem.

Adventurous, yet meaningful storylines told in rhythm and rhyme, accompanied by spectacular cinematic-like illustrations; provide the tomboyish main character with a marvelous opportunity to teach children valuable lessons, while entertaining at every turn.

These whimsical tales for boys and girls age 0 – 10 (to 110!), will break their world of imagination wide open, and transcend their hearts and souls beyond their wildest dreams.

In book four of the series, *The Kacklin' Kitchen*, Lilly the Lash finds herself in the quaint country village of Cobblestone Cove, where the insecure feelings of a young milk carton spawn outbursts of bullying behavior, leaving the important value of **RESPECT** hanging in the balance. Lilly, only ever seen by the reader, sends in a wise and compassionate cream cake to help the milk carton, and the others, understand how to successfully give and gain respect.

LEARNING ACTIVITIES

Be sure to check out Lilly's website **www.lillythelash.com** to find the array of **FREE** Lesson Plans, Crafting Activities, and Games created for various age ranges and multiple learning levels. These amazing activities are designed for the educational community in a classroom setting, as well as the family structure in a home environment.

DEDICATION

To my amazing parents
Robert and Ellen

If a child could dream a dream
of being loved in such a way in which
their precious little heart would be filled with
all the riches at the end of the rainbow...

they would be dreaming of YOU!

THE KACKLIN' KITCHEN

Book #4 in the Series
The Life and Times of Lilly the Lash®

A sweet summer's morning was just the right thing,
To supply the young birds with a song they could sing.
From a long crooked branch that reached out like a hand,
They had gathered together to strike up the band.

An audience grew, joining in on the fun,
Playing all of the instruments under the sun.

A cobblestone chimney, a few houses down,
Had offered Ms. Lilly the best seat in town.

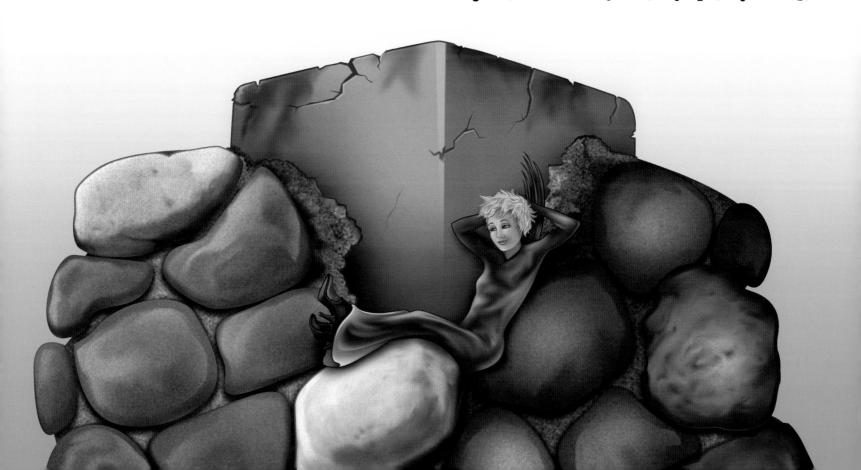

While resting her feet, Lilly happened to see,
Through a wide open window, the place she should be.
The eggs on the table were throwing a fit,
And the cheese and the butter were threatening to split!

She sprang from the roof top and raced in the room,
Whizzing past Bobbie the Beautiful Broom.
"I've had quite enough," Lilly heard Bobbie shout,

"If this
happens again,
he'd just

BETTER
LOOK
OUT!"

Lilly had only a moment to think,
Then circled around, locking eyes on the sink.
She spotted her target and dove in full force,
Unaware of the drip that would send her off course.

A large water droplet with Lilly inside,
Had her tumbling about like a carnival ride.
She had learned, by the time that the spoon broke her fall,
"When you leap, you must look, to avoid a close call."

So here's where I'll stop and explain in a flash,
How my life was empowered by Lilly the Lash.
This spirited eyelash had taken the role,
Of a teacher in waiting, to mentor my soul.

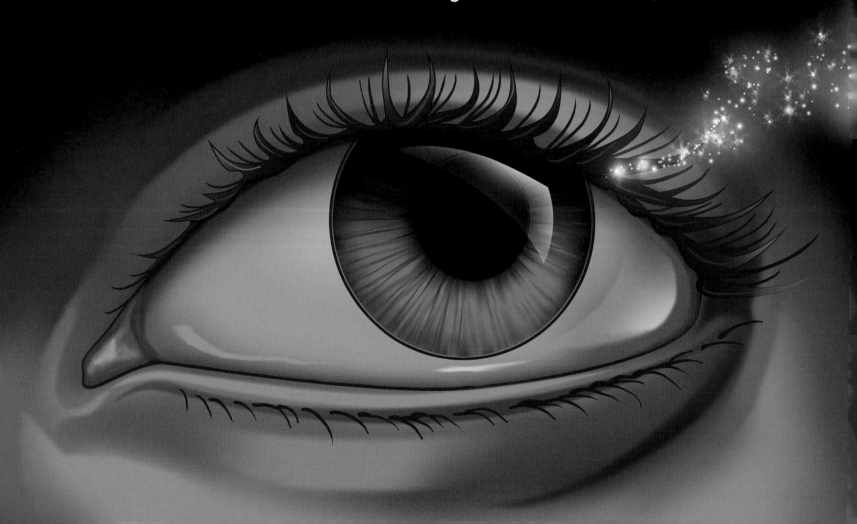

Lilly was special, she opened my mind,
To the deep understanding and love of mankind.
The secrets she shared helped to show me the way,
How to look towards the future, but care for today.

The words Lilly spoke were in riddle and rhyme,
Bringing lessons to light, which were there the whole time.
"The world," Lilly pointed, "is here at your feet,

ADMIT ONE

THE GREATEST SHOW ON EARTH

EVENT DATE: A LIFETIME
ENTRY FEE: PRICELESS
DON'T MISS THE EXCITEMENT

ADMIT ONE

In the sights and the sounds and the people you meet."

My Daily Thoughts

Then along came the day

when I knew in my heart,

That myself and Ms. Lilly

would soon come to part.

We both were convinced

by the work she had done,

That her message of goodness

could serve more than one.

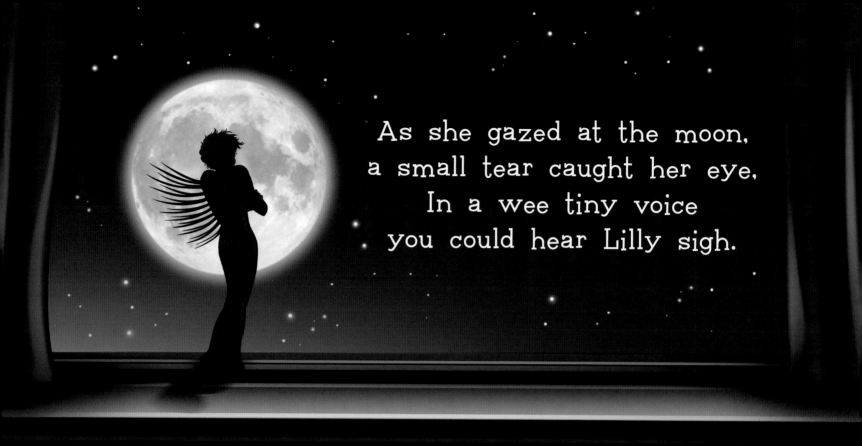

As she gazed at the moon,
a small tear caught her eye,
In a wee tiny voice
you could hear Lilly sigh.

Although I was sleeping, I felt a slight tug,
She had left me a gift, Lilly's best good-bye hug.

Well we better get hoppin' to that house on the hill,
Where Ms. Lilly's crawled onto the top of the sill.

A velvet-lined box with a decorative pin,
Was just open and waiting for her to move in.

When she turned to observe,
all the chatter would halt.
Not a word from Pam Pepper
or Sylvester the Salt.
Lilly took note
of what seemed to be strange,
Once the milk had arrived,
the whole atmosphere changed.

Everyone stood with concern on their face,
You could feel there was something about to take place.
A red and white carton named Mookee MaGee,
Was broadcasting loudly
"Hey, listen to me!"

"For all the new members I'd like to make clear,
That I'm the one running the show around here."
"Because I'm the BIGGEST"
he said with a taunt,
"Things happen exactly the way that I want."

Tea Anna peaked out from behind Rosie Cup,
She was trying not to shake, but indeed was shook up.

Mookee was pushing
her friend to the side,

And Bubba the Bread
felt the need to abide!

Most had experienced these intrusions before,
They'd come with the opening of the refrigerator door.
Once Mookee MaGee was set down in a spot,
He was rude to the others more often than not.

No one spoke out,
though they felt so abused,
This lack of response
left Ms. Lilly confused.

"They need to stand up," Lilly thought to herself,
"Because actions like these could endanger one's health."

Lilly heard footsteps approach from the hall,
It was Ellen, the owner, to make a quick call.
She phoned a close friend to find out how to make,
An extravagant, double-tiered, butter cream cake.

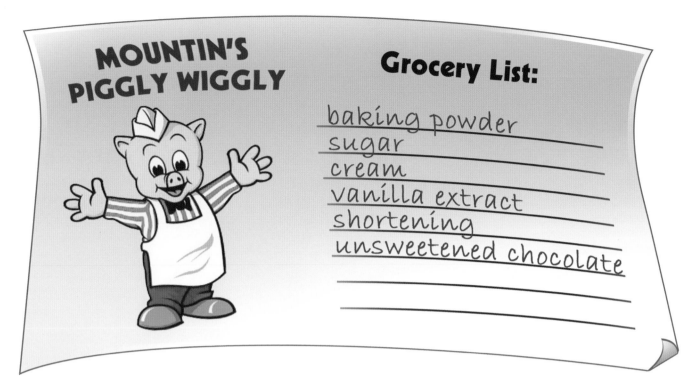

MOUNTIN'S PIGGLY WIGGLY

Grocery List:

baking powder
sugar
cream
vanilla extract
shortening
unsweetened chocolate

She tidied the kitchen while rushing around,
    Then made out her list, before heading to town.
As Ellen drove off, you could hear rants and raves,
    About Mookee MaGee and the way he behaves.

"It's absurd!" Chubby Cheddar cried out in distress,
"That we're allowing this bully to create all this stress.

We promise each time, to make 'that time' the last,
Then our confidence fades, and the moment flies past."

Rounding the corner while stretching his legs,
Young Eddie declared, "I can speak for the eggs.
We rally with honor and know what to do,

But when Mookee appears, we just don't follow through."

After watching this household dilemma unfold,
Ms. Lilly decided to take some control.
She worked out a plan that would surely reflect,
The importance of giving and receiving respect.

Entrees   Soups   Desserts   Appetizers

Double-Tiered Butter Cream Cake

1 Cup Flour
2 eggs

Humming a tune and lit up with a smile,
      Ellen returned to her recipe file.
She measured each morsel and stirred with delight,
      To create an exciting surprise for the night.

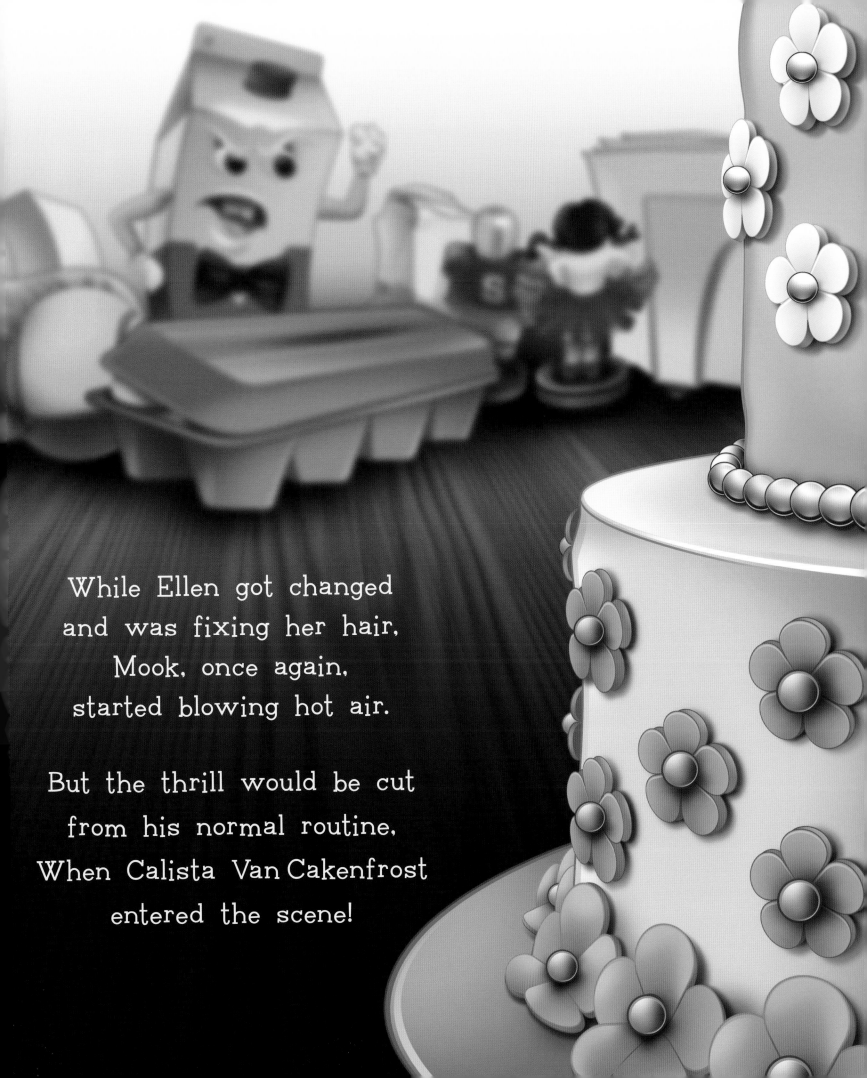

While Ellen got changed
and was fixing her hair,
Mook, once again,
started blowing hot air.

But the thrill would be cut
from his normal routine,
When Calista Van Cakenfrost
entered the scene!

Everyone stared with their mouths open wide,
As this mesmerizing marvel began speaking her mind.
"Tell me why, Mook MaGee, that you always prefer,
To make others feel bad, when that need not occur?"

"I've witnessed myself what goes on around here,
    And have come to believe that the cause may be fear.
My magnificent beauty is not from a dream,
    I was made by you ALL, not by one...but a team."

Double-Tiered Butter Cream Cake

1 Cup Flour	2 Teaspoons Baking Powder
3 Eggs	1 Cup Sugar
1 ½ Cups Milk	½ Teaspoon Salt
¾ Cup Butter	1 Tablespoon Vanilla Extract

Blend the flour, sugar, salt, and baking powder in a bowl.

Add the eggs, milk, butter, and vanilla extract.

Mix **ALL** of the ingredients together.

Calista then turned with a word of advice,
"To allow disrespect always comes with a price.
If you want to be treated with kindness and care,
Then you must take a stance, when you're treated unfair."

The silence that followed Calista's remark,
Had signaled Ms. Lilly her need to embark.
She grabbed for the satchel she cherished and praised,
Filled with the glow to grant hope in new ways.

Floating past Mookee, she dusted the sky,
With the glimmering flakes that would light up his eye.
This magical lash would take steps to provide,
The chance Mookee needed to flourish with pride.

All of a sudden
it clicked in his head,

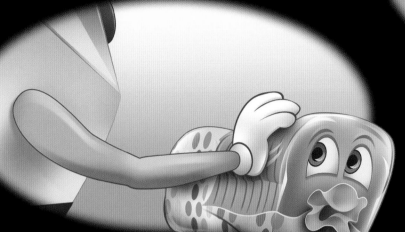

Mookee saw clearly
his actions brought dread.

He recognized trying to
act tough through his size,

Was nothing much more than a foolish disguise.

Approaching the group, he began to explain,
How his insecure feelings had caused so much pain.
"Please accept my apology that's long overdue,
"I'M SO SORRY," Mookee said, "and I'd like to start new."

Lilly looked on, as they welcomed their friend,
Bringing this story a true happy end.
She sat for a while, but would soon disappear,
She could only imagine where she'd venture from here.

The End

. . . are you sure?

FUN FACTS

 Carnivals are outdoor festivals offering games, rides, food, and a most cheerful atmosphere. Originating in Europe hundreds of years ago, these events were seen as a celebration of life, and were often based around a seasonal change. Let's Go!!!

 A diary is a book in which to record daily events. Hand written remarks document experiences, thoughts, and feelings of the writer. Considered private to many, diaries are sometimes tucked away, out of plain view. Where do you keep yours?!!

 Milk, according to many historians, has been used as a beverage for about 10,000 years. Although it looks rather creamy, surprisingly, it's mostly made of water. 90% of the entire planet's milk supply comes from dairy cows. Mmmmooooooooo!!!

 Tea cups are available in countless shapes and styles. Designed for serving tea and coffee, these delicate creations are collected around the world. Some folks buy them only in sets, while others prefer to select unique individual cups. Tea anyone?

 Cheddar cheese is pale yellow in color when initially produced, but is sometimes given an orange hue by using the seed from the Annatto tree. The author's home state of Wisconsin is one of the top producers of cheddar in the United States.

 Eggs produced by chickens are most often white or brown. Funny enough, it's their earlobe that determines the pigment. Hens with white earlobes lay white-shelled eggs, and hens with red earlobes lay brown-shelled eggs. Unique, huh?!?!!

 Cake decorating can be traced back to the 1600's, when elaborate desserts were presented at the feasts and celebrations of the very wealthy. Though sometimes offering a delectable treat...they were actually regarded more as a display piece.

 Vanilla extract is made from the vanilla bean. Farmed in Mexico, Tahiti, and Indonesia, it's one of the most expensive crops in the world to grow. It's great for baking, but can also be used to enhance drinks such as milk. Very tasty!!

 Refrigerators are common household appliances. Almost exclusively white until the mid-1950's, designers began to introduce such colors as turquoise and pink, with gold, green, and almond soon to follow. In the 1980's black was quite stylish, and stainless steel is a popular look of today. Do you know what color yours is?!!

Lilly's soarin' High
(High above the tree tops that is!)

The Life and Times of Lilly the Lash®
Jungle Jive

"Hop, Skip, and Jump!" cried out Teeder the Toad,
"For another 10 times, 'til the end of the road.
We'll strengthen the muscles that help us to play,
And wake up our minds for the start of the day."

Gathering short of the bank of the brook,
The gang took a rest to engage in a look.
Suddenly Derek slid down the mud slope,
Laughing as Hazel swung out on the rope!

Gliding along with the wind to her back,
Ms. Lilly had sensed she was on the right track.
She could feel the excitement that loomed in the air,
But detected the oncoming cloud of despair.

(Watch for Book #5 in this Series)

Follow Lilly on her next adventure to
Tree Bark Falls
Where a young monkey learns the important
Life Lesson of
BALANCE

SPECIAL THANKS

To Marc - The Illustrator

Or should I just call you Maestro?!
Thank you for making this book so much fun.
Your illustrations are so full of life, they allow children
to fully engage the characters in the story, and in turn,
learn the intended lesson with ease.
Brilliant I say! Just Brilliant!!!

To Elsa - My Designer and Friend

Book #4 Elsa!!! Can you believe it?
How totally and completely wonderful is that?!
Lilly's taking the world by storm, and you've been witness to it all.
It feels so good to be part of something so good,
with someone so good!
You're the best my friend!!

To My Exceptional Husband

Each day I share with you the journey that is Lilly the Lash,
and I bask in the knowledge that everything is exactly as it should be.
The strength of our bond allows Lilly to flourish within me.
Thank you for your extraordinary all-embracing love!!

To All of Lilly the Lash's Adoring and Inspiring Fans

From day one, the admiration, encouragement, and feedback we've received
from Lilly's fan base has overwhelmed and delighted us beyond belief.
Your sincere praises, heart-felt hugs,
and dizzying desire to spread Lilly's message to the world,
continue to confirm that we're on the right track.
We wouldn't be where we are today without **YOU!**
We want you to know how grateful we are for your loving support.
Your enthusiasm has molded this incredible sense of partnership,
and has left us with the profound understanding that

TOGETHER

WE'RE MAKING THE WORLD A BETTER PLACE!!!

Yahooooooooooooooooooooooooooooo!!!

Making Our World A Better Place

A percentage of the profit from
this book will go to the

ORGANIZATION FOR
AUTISM RESEARCH

For ALL of the amazing children and their extraordinary families.
Your struggle demands perseverance.
Your perseverance demands determination.
Your determination demands growth and change.

Your GROWTH and CHANGE demands a big whopping...

"WAY TO GO!!"